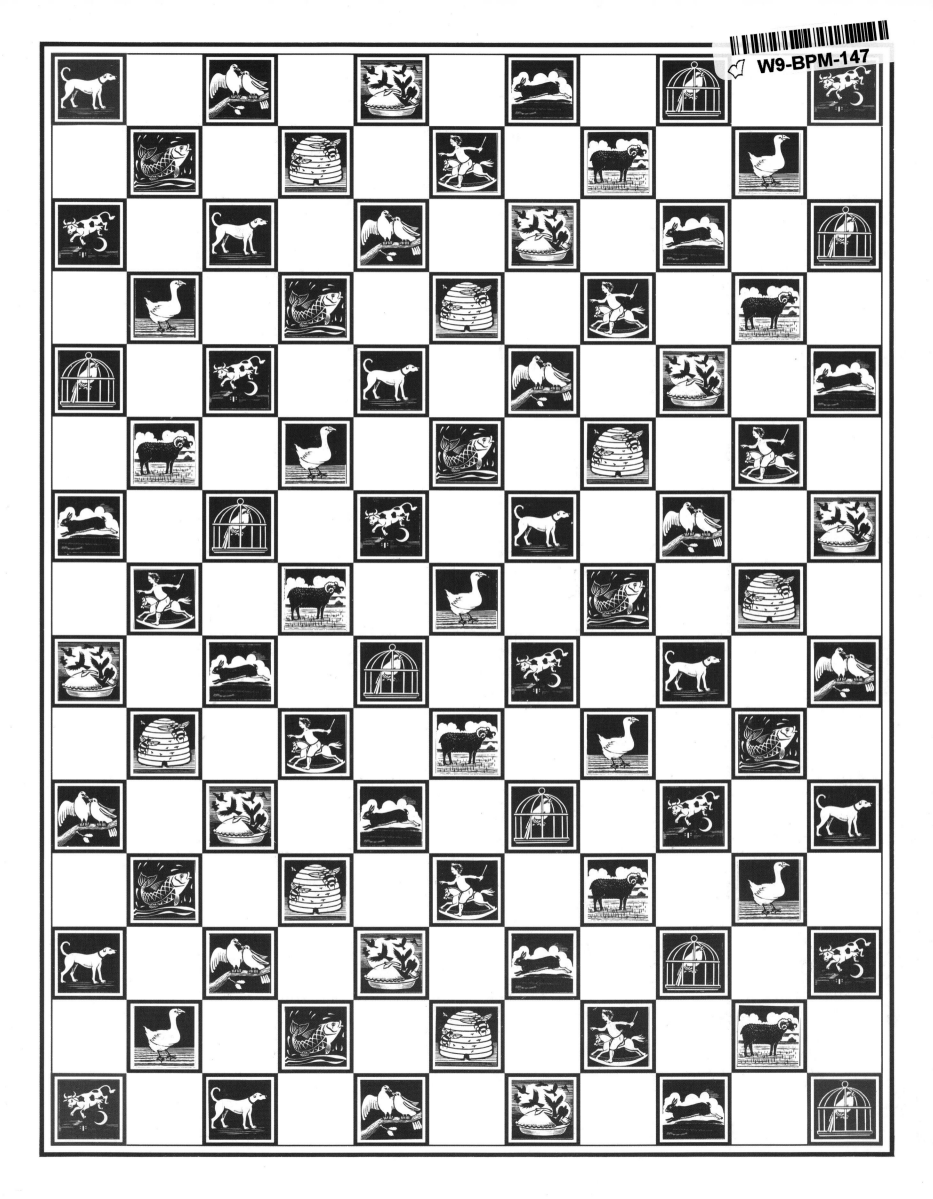

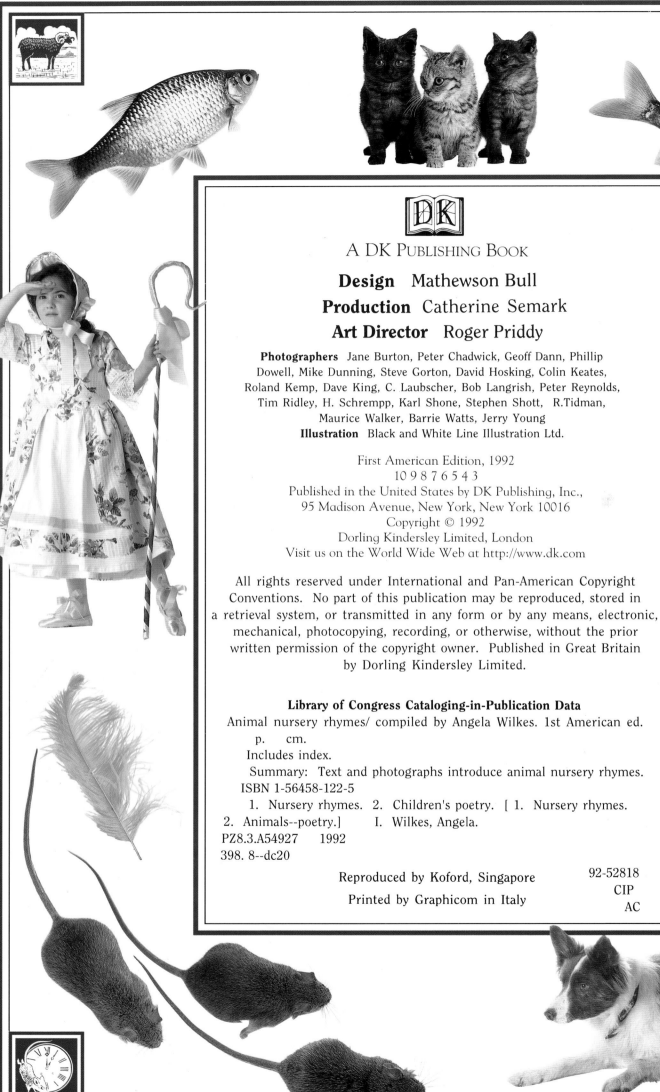

DK

A DK PUBLISHING BOOK

Design Mathewson Bull
Production Catherine Semark
Art Director Roger Priddy

Photographers Jane Burton, Peter Chadwick, Geoff Dann, Phillip Dowell, Mike Dunning, Steve Gorton, David Hosking, Colin Keates, Roland Kemp, Dave King, C. Laubscher, Bob Langrish, Peter Reynolds, Tim Ridley, H. Schrempp, Karl Shone, Stephen Shott, R.Tidman, Maurice Walker, Barrie Watts, Jerry Young
Illustration Black and White Line Illustration Ltd.

First American Edition, 1992
10 9 8 7 6 5 4 3
Published in the United States by DK Publishing, Inc.,
95 Madison Avenue, New York, New York 10016
Copyright © 1992
Dorling Kindersley Limited, London
Visit us on the World Wide Web at http://www.dk.com

Library of Congress Cataloging-in-Publication Data
Animal nursery rhymes/ compiled by Angela Wilkes. 1st American ed.
  p.   cm.
  Includes index.
  Summary: Text and photographs introduce animal nursery rhymes.
  ISBN 1-56458-122-5
  1. Nursery rhymes. 2. Children's poetry. [1. Nursery rhymes.
2. Animals--poetry.]   I. Wilkes, Angela.
PZ8.3.A54927   1992
398. 8--dc20
                                                    92-52818
Reproduced by Koford, Singapore   CIP
Printed by Graphicom in Italy   AC

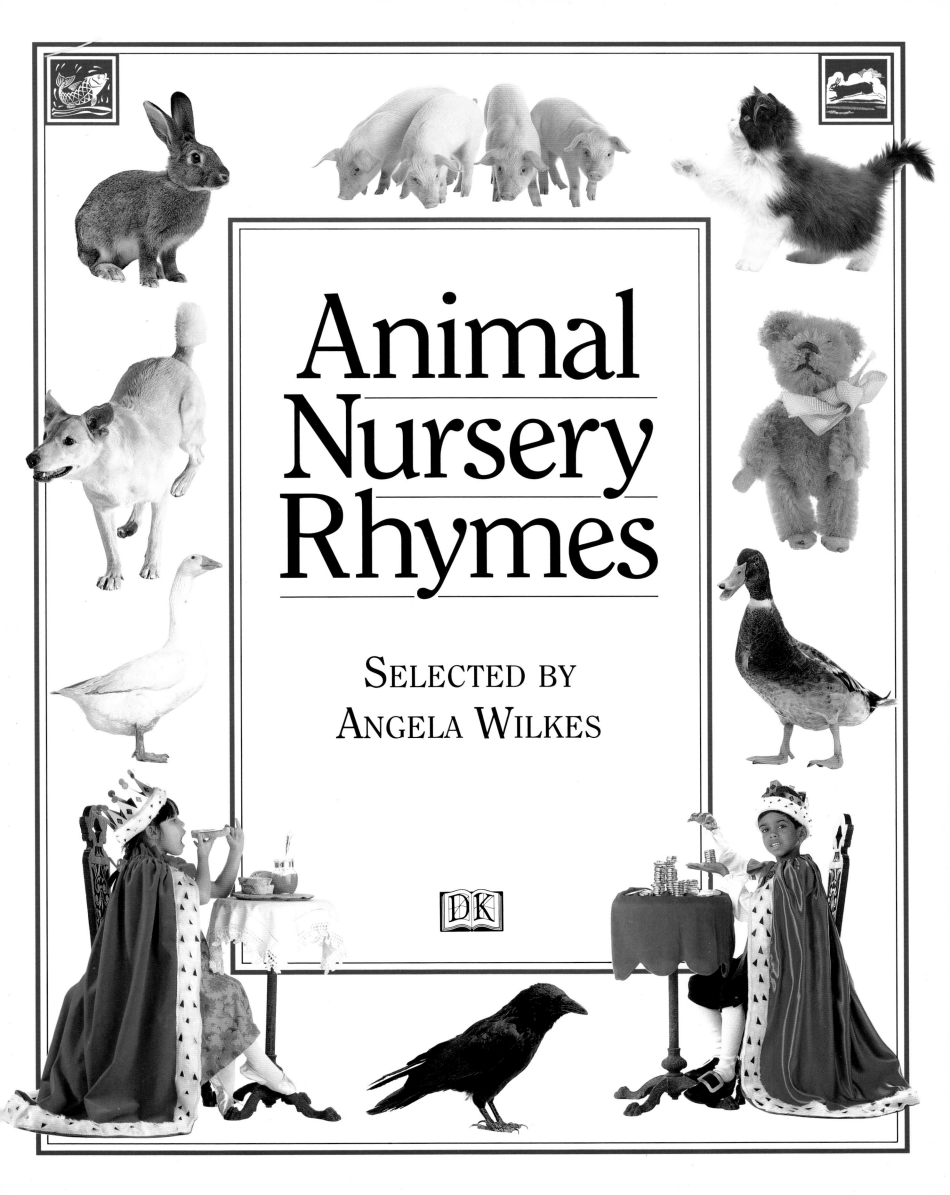

Animal
Nursery
Rhymes

SELECTED BY
ANGELA WILKES

CONTENTS

18

SING A
SONG OF
SIXPENCE

19

COCKCROW
I LOVE LITTLE PUSSY

20

YANKEE DOODLE
DAPPLE GRAY

21

WHERE IS HE?
I HAD TWO PIGEONS
THE GUINEA PIG

22

THREE LITTLE KITTENS

23

BOW-WOW

24

CUCKOO
THE NORTH WIND
ON THE FIRST OF MARCH

25

CHRISTMAS IS
COMING
A SWARM OF BEES IN MAY

26

FEATHERS
LITTLE FISHES
THREE BLIND MICE
TWO LITTLE DICKY BIRDS
ROUND THE GARDEN
SHOE A LITTLE HORSE

27

TWO LITTLE DOGS
BEE
ONE FOR SORROW
HEDGEHOG
FOXY
PARROT

28

THE HOUSE THAT
JACK BUILT

HUSH, LITTLE BABY

HUSH, little baby, don't say a word,
Papa's going to buy you a mockingbird.

IF the mockingbird won't sing,
Papa's going to buy you a diamond ring.

IF the diamond ring turns to brass,
Papa's going to buy you a looking glass.

IF the looking glass gets broke,
Papa's going to buy you a billy goat.

IF that billy goat runs away,
Papa's going to buy you another today.

BYE, BABY BUNTING

BYE, baby bunting,
Daddy's gone a-hunting,
Gone to get a rabbit skin
To wrap the baby
bunting in.

ONE, two, three, four, five,
Once I caught a fish alive,
Six, seven, eight, nine, ten,
Then I let it go again.
Why did you let it go?
Because it bit my finger so.
Which finger did it bite?
The little finger on the right.

THIS little pig went to market,
This little pig stayed at home,
This little pig had roast beef,
This little pig
had none,
And this little
pig cried,
"Wee-wee-wee-
wee-wee,"
all the way home.

HEY diddle, diddle,
The cat and the fiddle,
The cow jumped over the moon.
The little dog laughed
To see such fun,
And the dish ran away with
the spoon.

BAA, BAA, BLACK SHEEP

BAA, baa, black sheep,
Have you any wool?
Yes, sir, yes, sir,
Three bags full;

One for the master,
And one for the dame,
And one for the little boy
Who lives down the lane.

LITTLE MISS MUFFET

LITTLE Miss Muffet
Sat on a tuffet,
Eating her curds and whey;
Down came a spider,
Who sat down beside her
And frightened
Miss Muffet
away.

FISHES SWIM

FISHES swim in water clear,
Birds fly up into the air,
Serpents creep along the ground,
Boys and girls run round
and round.

HIGGLETY

HIGGLETY,
pigglety, pop!
The dog has
eaten the mop,
The pig's in a hurry,
The cat's in a flurry,
Higglety, pigglety, pop!

HICKORY, DICKORY

HICKORY,
dickory, dock,
The mouse ran
up the clock.
The clock struck one,
The mouse ran
down,
Hickory, dickory,
dock.

LITTLE BO-PEEP

LITTLE Bo-peep has lost her sheep,
And doesn't know where to find them;
Leave them alone, and they'll come home,
Bringing their tails behind them.

LITTLE Bo-peep fell fast asleep,
And dreamt she heard them bleating;
But when she awoke, she found it a joke,
For they were still a-fleeting.

THEN up she took her little crook,
Determined for to find them;
She found them indeed, but it made
her heart bleed,
For they'd left their tails behind them.

IT happened one day, as Bo-peep did stray
Into a meadow hard by,
There she espied their tails side by side,
All hung on a tree to dry.

SHE heaved a sigh, and wiped her eye,
And over the hillocks went rambling,
And tried what she could, as a
shepherdess should,
To tack again each to its lambkin.

BUTTERFLY

I'M a little butterfly
Born in a bower,
Christened in a teapot,
Flew in half an hour.

KINDNESS

IF I had a donkey that wouldn't go,
Would I beat him? Oh no, no.
I'd put him in the barn and give him some corn,
The best little donkey that ever was born.

LADYBUG

LADYBUG, ladybug,
Fly away home,
Your house is on fire
And your children
all gone;
All except one
And that's little Ann
And she has crept under
The frying pan.

LITTLE FRIEND

IN the greenhouse lives a wren,
Little friend of
little men;
When they're good
she tells them where
To find the apple,
quince, and pear.

MY BLACK HEN

HICKETY, pickety, my black hen,
She lays eggs for gentlemen;
Gentlemen come every day
To see what my black hen doth lay.

A TRAVELER

PUSSYCAT, pussycat,
Where have you been?
I've been to London
To look at the Queen.
Pussycat, pussycat,
What did you there?
I frightened a little
mouse under her
chair.

NIDDLE NODDLE

LITTLE Robin Redbreast
Sat upon a rail;
Niddle noddle went
his head,
Wiggle waggle
went his tail.

ITSY BITSY SPIDER

ITSY bitsy spider
Climbed up the water spout;
Down came the rain
And washed the spider out.
Out came the sun
And dried up all the rain,
And the itsy bitsy
spider
Climbed up the spout again.

TO THE BAT

BAT, bat, come under my hat,
And I'll give you a slice of bacon;
And when I bake, I'll give you a cake,
If I'm not mistaken.

WISE OWL

A wise old owl sat
in an oak.
The more he heard
the less he spoke.
The less he spoke
The more he heard.
Why can't we all be like
that wise old bird?

POLL PARROT

LITTLE Poll Parrot
Sat in his garret
Eating toast and tea;
A little brown mouse
Jumped into the house
And stole it all away.

TO THE SNAIL

SNAIL, snail, put out your horns,
And I'll give you bread and barleycorns.

MARY HAD A LITTLE LAMB

MARY had a little lamb,
Its fleece was white as snow;
And everywhere that Mary went
The lamb was sure to go.

IT followed her to school one day,
That was against the rule;
It made the children laugh and play
To see a lamb at school.

AND so the teacher turned it out,
But still it lingered near,
And waited patiently about
Till Mary did appear.

"WHY does the lamb love Mary so?"
The eager children cry;
"Why, Mary loves the lamb, you
know,"
The teacher did reply.

THE DOVE SAYS

THE Dove says, Coo, coo,
What shall I do?
I can scarce maintain two.
Pooh, pooh, says the wren,
I have ten,
And keep them all like
gentlemen.

Curr dhoo, curr dhoo
Love me, and I'll love you.

MRS. HEN

CHOOK, chook, chook, chook, chook,
Good morning, Mrs. Hen.
How many chickens have you got?
Madam, I've got ten.
Four of them are yellow,
And four of them
are brown,
And two of them are
speckled,
The nicest in the town.

Sing a Song of Sixpence

Sing a song of sixpence,
A pocket full of rye;
Four and twenty blackbirds,
Baked in a pie.

When the pie was opened,
The birds began to sing;
Wasn't that a dainty dish,
To set before
the King?

The King was in his counting-house,
Counting out his money;
The Queen was in the parlor,
Eating bread and honey.

The maid was in the garden,
Hanging out the clothes,
When down came a blackbird
And pecked off her nose.

COCKCROW

THE cock's on
the wood pile
Blowing his horn,
The bull's in the barn
A-threshing the corn,
The maids in the meadow
Are making the hay,
The ducks in the river
Are swimming away.

I LOVE LITTLE PUSSY

I love little pussy,
Her coat is so warm,
And if I don't hurt her
She'll do me no harm.
So I'll not pull her tail,
Nor drive her away,
But pussy and I
Very gently will play.
She shall sit by my side,
And I'll give her some food;
And pussy will love me
Because I am good.

YANKEE DOODLE

YANKEE Doodle came to town,
Riding on a pony;
He stuck a feather in his cap
And called it macaroni.

DAPPLE GRAY

I had a little pony,
His name was Dapple Gray,
His head was made of gingerbread,
His tail was made of hay;
He could amble, he could trot,
He could carry the mustard pot.
He could amble, he could trot,
Through the old town of Windsor.

WHERE IS HE?

OH where, oh where has my little
dog gone?
Oh where, oh where can he be?
With his ears cut short and his tail
cut long,
Oh where, oh where is he?

I HAD TWO PIGEONS

I had two pigeons bright and gay,
They flew from me the other day;
What was the reason they did go?
I cannot tell for
I do not know.

THE GUINEA PIG

THERE was a little guinea pig,
Who, being little, was not big;
He always walked upon his feet,
And never fasted when he eat.

WHEN from a place he ran away,
He never at that place did stay;
And while he ran, as I am told,
He never stood still for young or old.

HE often squeaked and sometimes
vi'lent,
And when he squeaked he never was
silent;
Though never instructed by a cat,
He knew a mouse was not a rat.

ONE day, as I am certified,
He took a whim and fairly died;
And as I'm told by men of sense,
He never has been living since.

THREE LITTLE KITTENS

THREE little kittens
They lost their mittens,
And they began to cry,
Oh, Mother dear,
We sadly fear
Our mittens we have lost.
What! lost your mittens,
You naughty kittens!
Then you shall have no pie.
Mee-ow, mee-ow, mee-ow.
No, you shall have no pie.

THE three little kittens
They found their mittens,
And they began to cry,
Oh, Mother dear,
See here, see here,
Our mittens we have found.
Put on your mittens,
You silly kittens,
And you shall have some pie.
Purr-r, purr-r, purr-r,
Oh, let us have some pie.

THE three little kittens
Put on their mittens
And soon ate up the pie;
Oh, Mother dear, we greatly fear
Our mittens we have soiled.
What! soiled your mittens,
You naughty kittens!
Then they began to sigh,
Mee-ow, mee-ow, mee-ow,
Then they began to sigh.

THE three little kittens
They washed their mittens,
And hung them out to dry;
Oh! Mother dear, do you not hear,
Our mittens we have washed.
What! washed your mittens,
Then you're good kittens,
But I smell a rat close by.
Mee-ow, mee-ow, mee-ow,
We smell a rat close by.

BOW-WOW

BOW-WOW, says the dog,
Mew, mew, says the cat,
Grunt, grunt, goes the hog,
And squeak goes the rat.
Tu-whu, says the owl,
Caw, caw, says the crow,
Quack, quack, says the duck,
And what cuckoos say, you know.

CUCKOO

THE cuckoo comes in April,
He sings his song in May;
In the middle of June
He changes his tune,
And then he flies away.

THE NORTH WIND

THE north wind doth blow,
And we shall have snow,
And what will poor Robin do then,
Poor thing?
He'll sit in a barn,
And keep himself warm,
And hide his head under his wing,
Poor thing.

ON THE FIRST OF MARCH

ON the first of March
The crows begin to search;
By the first of April they are sitting still;
By the first of May
They've all flown away,
Coming greedy back again
With October's wind
and rain.

CHRISTMAS IS COMING

CHRISTMAS is coming,
The geese are getting fat,
Please to put a penny
In the old man's hat.
If you haven't got a penny,
A ha'penny will do;
If you haven't got a ha'penny,
Then God bless you!

A SWARM OF BEES IN MAY

A swarm of bees in May
Is worth a load of hay.

A swarm of bees in June
Is worth a silver spoon.

A swarm of bees in July
Is not worth a fly.

FEATHERS

CACKLE, cackle, Mother Goose,
Have you any feathers loose?
Truly have I, pretty fellow,
Half enough to
fill a pillow.
Here are
quills, take
one or two,
And down to make
a bed for you.

LITTLE FISHES

LITTLE fishes in a brook,
Father caught them on a hook,
Mother fried them in a pan,
Johnnie eats them
like a man.

THREE BLIND MICE

THREE blind mice, see how they run!
They all ran after the farmer's wife,
Who cut off their tails with a carving knife,
Did you ever see such a thing in your life,
As three blind mice?

TWO LITTLE DICKY BIRDS

TWO little dicky birds,
Sitting on a wall;
One named Peter
The other named Paul.
Fly away, Peter!
Fly away, Paul!
Come back, Peter!
Come back,
Paul!

ROUND THE GARDEN

ROUND and round
the garden
Like a teddy bear;
One step, two step,
Tickle you
under there!

SHOE A LITTLE HORSE

SHOE a little horse,
Shoe a little mare,
But let the little colt
Go bare, bare, bare.

TWO LITTLE DOGS

TWO little dogs sat by the fire
Over a fender of coal-dust;
Said one little dog
To the other little dog,
If you don't talk,
Why, I must.

BEE

LITTLE bird of Paradise
She works her work
both neat and nice,
She pleases God,
She pleases man,
She does the work
that no man can.

ONE FOR SORROW

ONE for sorrow, two for joy,
Three for a girl, four for a boy,
Five for silver, six for gold,
Seven for a secret never
to be told.

HEDGEHOG

LITTLE Billy Breek
Sits by the creek,
He has more horns
Than all the king's
sheep.

FOXY

PUT your finger in Foxy's hole,
Foxy's not at home.
Foxy's at the back door,
Picking a marrow bone.

PARROT

CLOTHED in yellow, red, and green,
I chat before the King and Queen;
Of neither house nor land possessed,
By lords and knights I am caressed.

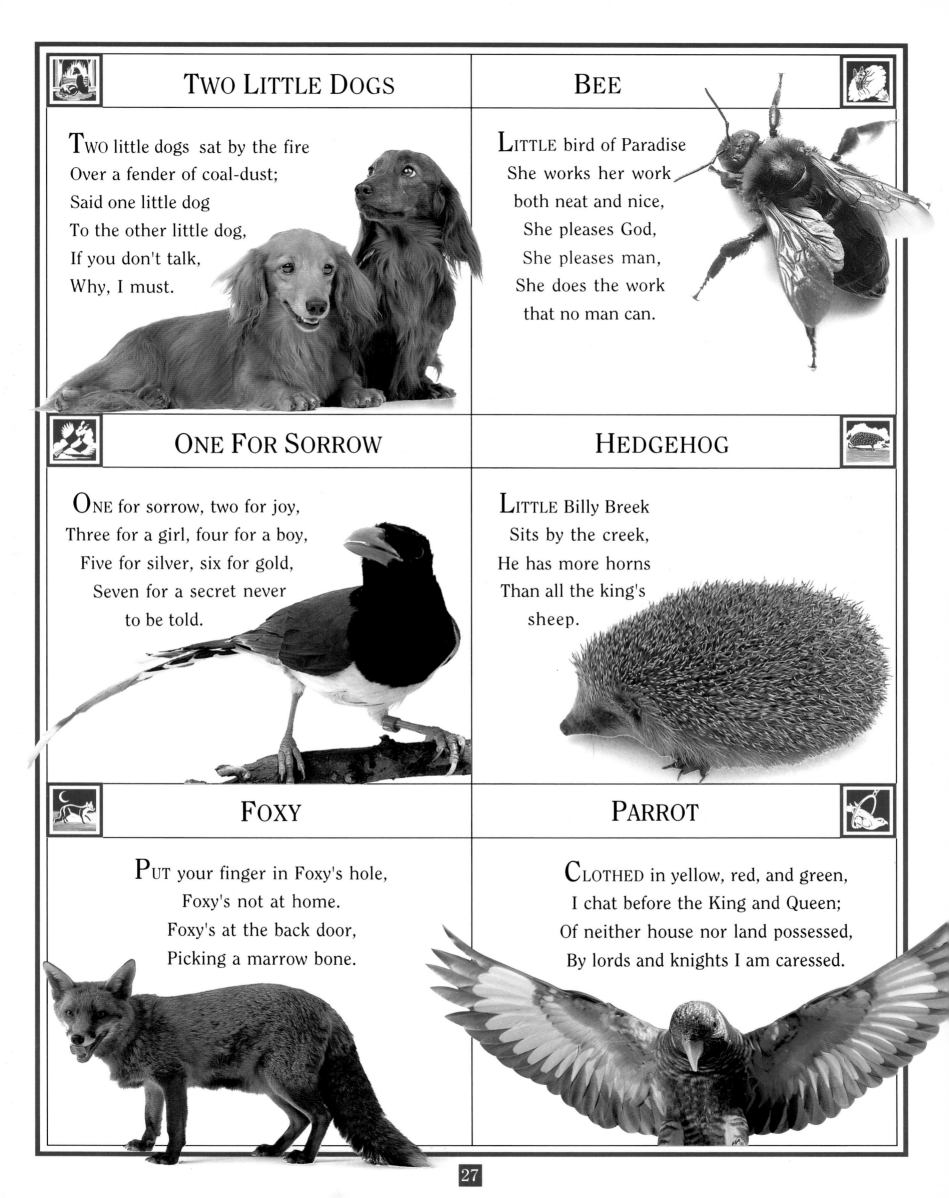

THE HOUSE THAT JACK BUILT

THIS is the house
that Jack built.

THIS is the malt
That lay in the house
that Jack built.

THIS is the rat,
That ate the malt
That lay in the house
that Jack built.

THIS is the cat,
That killed the rat,
That ate the malt
That lay in the house
that Jack built.

THIS is the dog,
That worried the cat,
That killed the rat,
That ate the malt
That lay in the house
that Jack built.

THIS is the cow with the crumpled horn,
That tossed the dog,
That worried the cat,
That killed the rat,
That ate the malt
That lay in the house
that Jack built.

THIS is the maiden all forlorn,
That milked the cow with the crumpled horn,
That tossed the dog, that worried the cat,
That killed the rat, that ate the malt
That lay in the house
that Jack built.

THIS is the man all tattered and torn,
That kissed the maiden all forlorn,
That milked the cow with the crumpled horn,
That tossed the dog, that worried the cat,
That killed the rat, that ate the malt
That lay in the house
that Jack built.

THIS is the priest all shaven and shorn,
That married the man all tattered and torn,
That kissed the maiden all forlorn,
That milked the cow with the crumpled horn,
That tossed the dog, that worried the cat,
That killed the rat, that ate the malt
That lay in the house
that Jack built.

THIS is the cock that crowed in the morn,
That waked the priest all shaven and shorn,
That married the man all tattered and torn,
That kissed the maiden all forlorn,
That milked the cow with the crumpled horn,
That tossed the dog, that worried the cat,
That killed the rat, that ate the malt
That lay in the house
that Jack built.

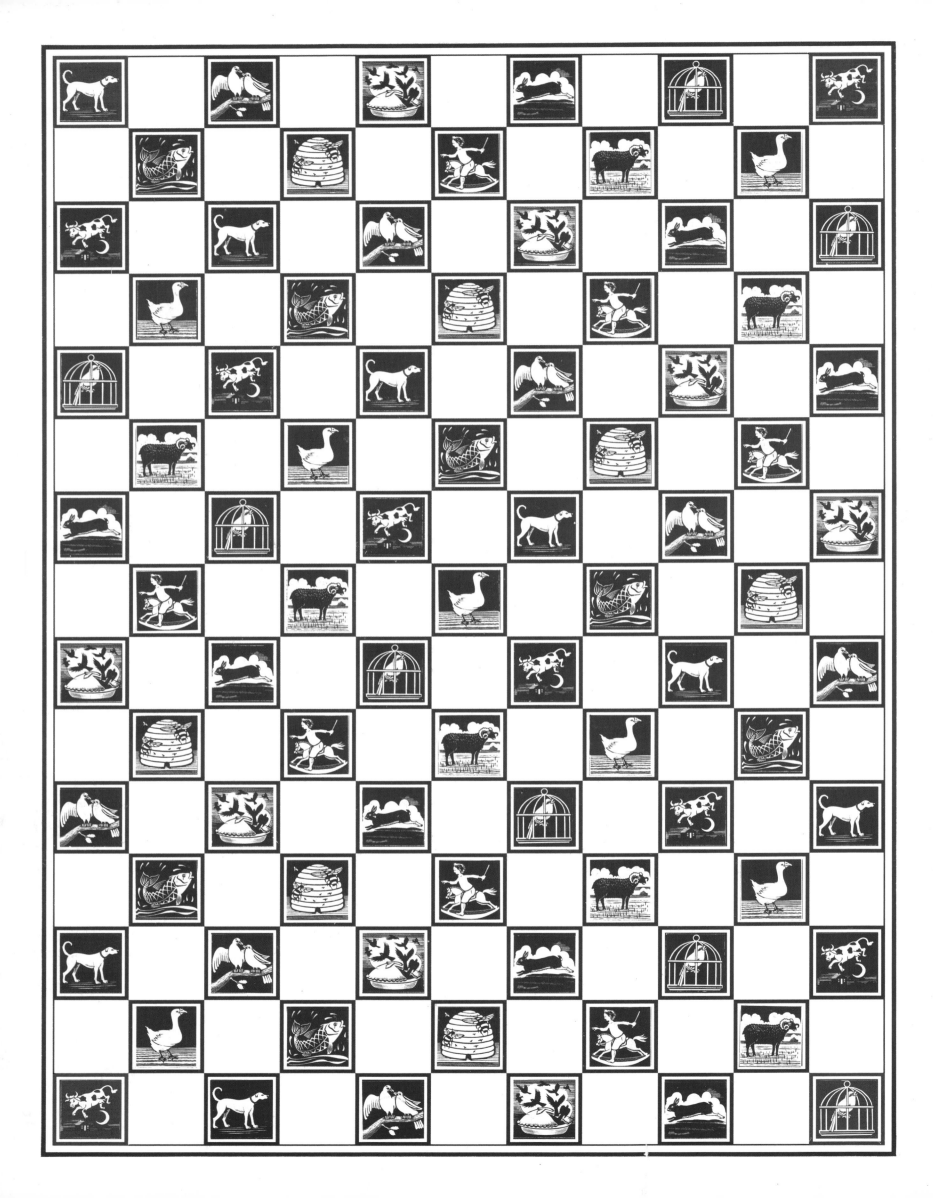